Dedicated to my grandkids:
Evan, Logan, Hunter, Ellis

Illustrated by Will Orr

I started small,
but then I grew

So many things
I learned to do

I learned to crawl,
then learned to walk

I learned to climb
and learned to talk.

And as I grew,
I learned to play

And now I play
most every day

But still I learn
and still I grow

So many things
I need to know

It will take years
before I'm through

I started small,
but then I grew.

The End.